For Whitehill School,
with love and happy memories - SAH
For Amy - MM

A Red Fox Book

Published by Random House Children's Books
20 Vauxhall Bridge Road, London SW1V 2SA

A division of the Random House Group Ltd
London Melbourne Sydney Auckland
Johannesburg and agencies throughout the world

1 3 5 7 9 10 8 6 4 2

First published in Great Britain by Red Fox 2001

Published in hardback by Heinemann Library, a division of
Reed Educational and Professional Publishing Limited,
by arrangement with Random House Children's Books

Printed in Singapore by Tien Wah Press

THE RANDOM HOUSE GROUP Limited Reg. No. 954009
www.randomhouse.co.uk

ISBN 0 09 941728 6 (paperback)
ISBN 0 431 02413 8 (hardback)

Shadowhog

Sandra Ann Horn

Mary McQuillan

RED FOX

Time to wake up!

Motherhog watched the sky. When the
moon was full, she woke her children up.
She washed their faces and whispered,
"Wake up, my prickly dears. The lantern
moon is shining. The slithery slugs are out.
It's suppertime."

5

Roly and Shuffle scurried out of the nest into the moonlit garden, but Pippin put his nose out and went no further.

Something was wrong. He could see everything twice!

Wait for me!

It's scary out there!

Help!

The flowers and
bushes, the garden shed
and the wheelbarrow all
had a dark mysterious
twin lurking beside them.

Then someone shone a torch round the garden and called, "Kitty, kitty, kitty!"

The dark mysterious twins all jumped about. They grew big, and small, and changed places all of a sudden.

"Help!" squeaked Pippin.
He closed his eyes tight and put his
paws over them.

Then he rolled into a ball.

"Oh, come out of that ball," said Motherhog, "and you'll see how nice it is outside. It's full of suppery things for hungry hedgehogs."

"No," said Pippin, "I won't. I'm scared!"

"Don't you want your supper?"

Pippin unrolled a little bit. "Yes," he said.

"But what about the jumping things?"

"Nonsense, dear," said Motherhog. "Out you come."

Motherhog set off
across the garden with Roly and Shuffle
trundling behind, but Pippin stayed in the
nest with his tummy empty.

12

When Motherhog and the others came
back, they were as full and round as
the moon.

"You'll have to come tomorrow night," said
Motherhog. "Hedgehogs have to eat until
they're as fat as ever they can be, or they
won't be able to sleep through the winter."

"I'll try," said Pippin.

When the daylight came, they were all asleep except Pippin. He was too hungry to sleep and, besides, he had been thinking.

"I will find my food in the day," he thought, "when those jumpy things aren't in the garden."

He put his nose out of the nest and
looked around. The sky was cloudy.
There were no dark twins in the garden.
Pippin set off across the lawn.

He hadn't gone far when he smelled a
wonderful smell and saw a round white dish
on the ground. He put his nose over the
edge of it.

"Yum! Dinner!" he said.
At the very same moment, another
nose arrived at the dish.

A sharp black nose with long
whiskers, two big green eyes and
a furry face.

Are you my supper?

Two ginger ears pricked up.
A pink tongue poked out.
Pippin saw sharp teeth.

19

Pippin's prickles stood right on end and
he rolled into a ball quicksmart.
His heart beat tickatickatickatick.
He felt the fox patting him.

He rolled up even tighter.
The fox cried, OW!

OW! OW!

OW!

Pippin peeped out, and saw the fox running away, holding up his hurt paw. "Ha! I prickled him!" said Pippin. He snatched some food and scuttled back home.

I want my MUM!

He tumbled in on
top of the others,
and woke them up.

"Where have you been?" said Motherhog. "Don't you know it's dangerous for hedgehogs to be out in the day?"

"I do now," said Pippin. "Something nasty with a ginger face and sharp teeth tried to get me."

"Oh, dear," said Motherhog, "that was a
fox! Promise me you'll never go out in the
day again. You could have been killed!"

"I promise," said Pippin. Then he fell
asleep, still hungry.

When the moon was high, Motherhog woke
her children up. "Suppertime," she said.
"Off we go."

She bustled them out of the nest. Pippin
took two steps forward and stopped.

The dark twins were
in the garden again.

Pippin started to creep home, backwards.

But something was creeping along beside him! It was round and spiky. Pippin stopped. The spiky thing stopped.

Pippin looked out of
the corner of his eye.
"Please go away,"
he whispered.

The spiky thing did not go away.

"W-who are you?" said Pippin. "And why are you following me?"

The spiky thing
did not answer.

A motorcycle went
by the garden gate.

The spiky thing GREW.

"Help!" squealed Pippin.
Motherhog came trundling back.
"What now?" she puffed.
"There!" said Pippin. "Make it go away!"

"Oh, that's only your moonshadow,"
said Motherhog, and she sang:

Hedgehogs and Shadowhogs
come out to play,
the moon does shine
as bright as day.

"Come on," said Motherhog. "I'll show you
how to play shadowpuppets. You stand up
on your back legs and put your prickles
flat. Now put one arm like this and one like
that. See?"

Pippin looked at the shed wall. There was a shadowteapot.

They made a shadowrabbit and a shadowbird.
Then they did some shadowboxing.

The fox came creeping, very low and
very slow. Pippin and Motherhog did not
see him. They were playing shadow
shrinking and growing against the wall.
They had just got to the growing part, and
Pippin's shadow was HUGE.

The fox saw
gigantic
shadowprickles.

Suddenly, he remembered his hurt paw.
He ran out of the garden and down the road,
so fast that he overtook a motorcycle.
"Yi, yi, yi!" he howled,
all the way home.

Pippin and Motherhog laughed until they rolled over.

Ho ho ho!

Hee hee hee!

Then they went on a slug and beetle hunt until Pippin was nearly full. They played hide-and-seek in and out of the moonshadows.

When the moon went down and the moonshadows began to disappear, Pippin and Motherhog trundled home. The others were already in the nest.

"Where have you been?" asked Roly.

"What have you been doing?" asked Shuffle. "I've had my supper twice and I've scared a fox and I've played with the moonshadows," said Pippin. "And I'm going to do it all again tomorrow night. I'm not a scaredyhog any more!"

Play shadow shrinking and growing like Pippin and his mum.

You will need: paper, scissors, a pencil, sticky tape, a torch

1. Draw a shape, such as a star or a flower, and cut it out. Attach it to a pencil with sticky tape.

2. Make the room as dark as you can. Stand next to a wall and shine the torch onto your shape. See the shadow it makes.

3. Hold the shape near the torch light. How big is the shadow now?

4. Move your shape away from the torch. Is the shadow bigger or smaller?

5. In the story, when the motorcycle zooms by, Pippin's shadow grows HUGE. Zoom the torch close to the bottom of your shape and away again. What happens?

You can make shadow shapes on your wall with your hands.

1. Make a circle with your thumb and first finger. Hold your other fingers up straight with the second finger bent a little bit forwards.

Shine the torch on your hand. What does the shadow look like? Can you make it talk?

2. Hold up two hands with your thumbs together and your fingers spread out. If someone shines the torch on your hands, what does the shadow look like? Can you make it fly?

What other shadow shapes can you make?

Play games with your shadow on a sunny day outside. Can you shake hands with a friend's shadow if your hands are not touching?

Shadows are dark or shaded areas where objects stop light.

Can you hide your shadow?

45

Sandra Ann Horn

Have you ever met a hedgehog? Hedgehogs come out at night and they are really small, so it isn't easy to see them. Luckily, they are *very* noisy. One night in my back garden, I heard a loud snorky snuffly noise, and when I looked to see what it was, it was a hedgehog!

Were you scared of the dark when you were little? I was a bit scared of the dark, when I couldn't see *anything* at all, but it isn't often that dark. After a while, your eyes get used to it and you can see all sorts of things.

How did you get the idea for this story? Once, when I was small, my brothers and I were creeping about in the dark with a torch. We started to creep upstairs. My dad had left his hat on the post at the bottom of the stairs. As we walked up and the torch moved, the shadow of the post suddenly flew up the wall very fast and it looked like a tall man in a hat. I thought of this when I wrote *Shadowhog*.

What do you do when you get stuck on a story? I have a group of writing friends. We eat chocolate biscuits and read our work to each other. Often, one of my friends makes a helpful suggestion and it unsticks me.

Mary McQuillan

Meet the illustrator.

Hey, that's me!

How did you paint the pictures in this book? I used a mixture of paint and acrylic inks. I painted all the pictures at once and it took about ten weeks.

Did you draw when you were a child? Yes, I still remember wearing a little apron and standing in front of a drawing board, sloshing paints over the paper and me. I'm still doing it now!

What did you like to do when you were little? What did you hate most? I loved splashing about in puddles in my little red wellies and making things out of bits of household junk and modelling clay. I hated having to stop playing and go to bed.

Do you have any pets? I live with a dog called Bonzo. He sleeps in my workroom all day and snores so loudly that I have to turn up the radio so I can hear the songs.

Bonzo is thinking up a story. Can you think of one?

Can I be an illustrator like you? Yes, of course. Just keep drawing and painting. Practise by drawing your pets or your family and using your imagination.

Let your ideas take flight with
Flying Foxes

All the Little Ones – and a Half
by Mary Murphy

Sherman Swaps Shells
by Jane Clarke and Ant Parker

Digging for Dinosaurs
by Judy Waite and Garry Parsons

Shadowhog
by Sandra Ann Horn and Mary McQuillan

The Magic Backpack
by Julia Jarman and Adriano Gon

Jake and the Red Bird
by Ragnhild Scamell and Valeria Petrone